DIVORCE AFTER FIFTY AIN'T NO DISGRACE, BUT IT AIN'T NO HONOR EITHER

By
Norma Lewis

PublishAmerica
Baltimore

ISBN: 1-4137-8260-4
PUBLISHED BY PUBLISHAMERICA, LLLP
www.publishamerica.com
Baltimore

Printed in the United States of America

CONTENTS

DEDICATION

This book is lovingly dedicated to my two sons, Bill Lewis, II, and Todd Lewis, who think their mom can do anything and have me almost convinced that I can.

ACKNOWLEDGMENTS

I want to thank the following people for their help and encouragement with my writing:

Roberta Simpson Brown, my writer friend and mentor, who helped, encouraged, and believed in me through the years. Because I am an analog woman in a digital world, her cyber skills made it possible for me finally to see my book in print.

Nancy Gall-Clayton, my very own cheerleader, who inundated me with notices of writing competitions from the Erma Bombeck Writing Competition to Women Who Write Contest to keep me honing my skills while continuing to work on my book.

All my friends, relatives, and fellow members of the Cherokee Round Table writers' group, who supported and motivated me not to give up on my book.

PROLOGUE

I was divorced in 1973 after twenty-five years of marriage. Being in a couple-oriented society, I felt more than divorced. I felt dismembered. But as time went on, I learned to function as a single person and my thinking changed. I felt unfettered—free to think and do as I pleased.

Divorce is likened to an ill wind that blows some good. Living alone may be hard at first, but what's really great is that you find out you can do it.

I'm not going to write a *hernia special* –i.e., a James Michener *five pounder* on the subject. I am going to share some observations and experiences of mine. Maybe you can relate. Maybe they'll make you laugh. Being divorced after fifty ain't no disgrace. It doesn't mean you're a failure. It just means it wasn't working anymore.

One thing for sure is that you won't die from divorce. However, your knee-jerk reaction is to change your will. Delete the husband and leave everything to the kids or the dog.

That's not the end of it. There's life after divorce. Time passes and the next time you work on your will, it may be at a pre-nuptial agreement, should you take the plunge again.

And see? Life goes on.

WIDOW OR GRASS WIDOW

When he asked me for a divorce, I should've shot him. I probably would've just gotten a prison sentence. I'd have had three square meals a day that I didn't have to prepare and no more wondering about what to wear everyday.

Time passes quickly and people tend to forget. When I served my time, I could always have moved away. No one would've known I was a jailbird widow.

However, the basic widow is treated differently. It just smacks of respectability, and sympathy is rampant. *Hey, it's not her fault she's single!* Nobody asks whose fault it was. There are no questions to answer. The widow could've had a marriage made in hell, but now she's doin' fine and didn't have to go through the hassle of divvying up the assets.

When the spouse has gone to meet his maker, he's *really* gone. But when there's a divorce, that's a different story. It's a death of a marriage and you keep running into the corpse.

Back in the 20s and 30s, there weren't too many divorcees around. They were called *Grass Widows.* When I was a little girl and overheard in hushed tones *She's a grass widow*, it lent an air of mystery and intrigue—the Mata Hari mystique. I even thought all grass widows wore trench coats.

Now I'm a big girl. Looking back, I now understand the hushed tones. They were the same tones used when it's said someone has a social disease.

In spite of all this, I am still prone to clinging to my childhood impressions of what I thought a grass widow was. I own a dynamite London Fog trench coat. I look and feel great in it! Who knows? There may be mystery and intrigue in my future, and, if there is, I'm dressed for it!

MARRIAGE IS LOVE—DIVORCE IS WAR

When I went looking for a lawyer to take my case, I remembered Zsa Zsa Gabor's mother being quoted as saying, "When you lie down with dogs, you get up with fleas." If that kind of philosophy was good enough for the Gabors, it was good enough for me. It fit in with my philosophy: *Don't stoop to conquer.* No cut throat lawyers for me. I had to live with myself.

However, since a lawyer works for himself, who's watching the lawyer? The State Bar Association and the Yellow Pages don't tell you a thing. He could be so crooked that, when he died, they'd have to screw him into the ground to bury him. All you've got is his name and phone number and your blind faith.

The first lawyer I met with threw bubble gum balls in the air and caught them with remarkable accuracy like a seal going for a fish as I was leaving his office. He was a junior partner in the firm. I thought he was too carefree and let him go. I found out later that his entire family was composed of top-notch lawyers and, today, he is a prominent Senator. I've since had occasion to work with him and he has earned my respect. He was the one I should've had. But I digress.

As I was leaving the office of the second lawyer after telling him my story, he said, "We'll crucify him!" I automatically eliminated him. I didn't want to have to hear my husband say that I had taken him to the cleaners when, in reality, the only time I ever took him to the cleaners was when his car wasn't working. I gave him a ride to the Chinese laundry where he met a fellow Jaycee to attend a meeting.

I picked the third lawyer because he was a nice guy. I found out that the old saying is really true: *Nice guys finish last.* He was everybody's friend. I didn't want a killer, but I needed a fighter.

When I got to court, I realized that the passion that brings two people together is the same passion that is present when the two split up. Previously, my only exposure to the law was traffic court. If tears didn't get it in traffic court, you were dead in divorce court. You'd have to have a stroke or a seizure.

I should've had a good, strong lawyer who would fight harder for me, and a psychiatrist who would reassure me that I was not a bitch for asking for financial security for my remaining years. I also learned that finding a lawyer to please everyone was like getting into a piss fight with a skunk. It's a no-win situation.

NO-FAULT DIVORCE

The no-fault divorce law states that both shall live in the same manner to which each was accustomed. They got that right! I know I am!

I'm *still* taking out the garbage, doing laundry, cooking meals, grocery shopping, stopping by the liquor store, and picking up charcoal for the weekend. Only the numbers have changed. Now I'm doing it for one instead of four. My lifestyle hasn't changed at all. Neither has his.

He's *still* boogying, playing poker, playing golf, going to the track, and stopping off at the local watering hole on his way home from work.

With no-fault divorce, assets are to be divided evenly. The lawyers handle all the financial aspects, while the couple submits a list of what they want to keep in the line of furniture, cars, and the like. There ought to be a training manual for this part!

I only wish I had known that Lean Cuisine was going to be invented. I never would have gone for the pots and pans that were already twenty-five years old and looked like something you'd take camping. I would have opted for the washer and dryer.

AT LAST I'VE GOT MY OWN ROOM

Until I became divorced, I never realized that I'd never lived alone in my entire life. I spent the early part of my life in Connecticut living with an aunt and uncle who had two boys and a girl. I shared a room with their daughter Bette.

Our room had a slanted ceiling and one window with a sheer white curtain always blowing in over the windowsill like an Andrew Wyeth painting. We had a white iron bed, a braided rug, a small rocking chair, an oak dresser, and a large armoire for our clothes.

Shortly after I graduated from high school, we were in World War II and I went to work in the Field Services Office at Pratt and Whitney Aircraft in East Hartford, Connecticut, which was thirty miles from home. Because of gasoline rationing, I had to share an apartment in Hartford with a schoolteacher and go home on weekends.

Her apartment had a kitchen, living room, and sunroom that was filled with a gargantuan grand piano. My roommate also gave private music lessons in her apartment. The living room was furnished with many lovely antiques. At one end of the room was a dark, solid wall of wood carved with intricate designs. Behind this wall was a Murphy bed for the schoolteacher.

At one end of the kitchenette, in the corner, was a desk, chair, and a day bed covered with a paisley shawl from India. That's where I slept. No closets, no doors, no privacy, no bedroom.

Overcome with patriotic fervor and wanting to do my bit, I enlisted in the WAVES and ended up in Naval Intelligence and had more roommates than I could count. I took my boot camp training at Hunter College in New York, shipping out for training at Iowa State Teachers' College in Cedar Falls, Iowa, and reported for duty in a Naval Intelligence Unit in Charleston, South Carolina. In all three places, the décor was the same—four wooden lockers and four green double-decker bunks. The only difference was that there were actual rooms with doors in the colleges, but at my duty station, there were cubicles with no doors, similar to the room dividers found in today's business offices.

After the war, I enrolled in Moravian College for Women--more roommates. The furniture in the dorms belied the fact that it was one of the finest women's colleges in the east. It was your basic, scarred, maple twin bed, dresser, desk, and chair. Each room had two roommates going nuts with creativity and accessories, ranging from stuffed animals to dead prom corsages dangling from their bulletin boards.

While in school, I met and fell in love with a World War II veteran who was attending a men's college in the next town. We married and roomed together for twenty-five years, sharing a bedroom filled with Early American style rock maple furniture.

Now that I'm actually living alone for the first time in fifty years, I've had to endure remarks from all my friends concerning my bedroom, awash with a white eyelet bed spread, pillows and curtains, and white wicker furniture. The most common comment was that it looked like a little girl's room. Is there something Freudian here because I never had a room of my own or what?

IF A TREE FALLS IN THE FOREST AND NOBODY HEARS IT, IS THERE A SOUND?

Being single again after fifty ain't so bad. It's kinda like hanging. You get used to hanging if you hang long enough. The bright side is that you can do anything you want by yourself.

At work, I'd hear the end of the week mantra chanted by my co-workers: *Thank God it's Friday*. For most, it meant a big weekend ahead. All Friday meant to me was that in two days it would be Monday.

Some wild Friday nights, I'd curl up in front of the TV with a can of Hershey chocolate syrup, a spoon, and a jar of peanut butter. I'd dip the spoon in the peanut butter and roll it around in the chocolate and eat ad nauseum. Some people woke up with hangovers on Saturday morning. I woke up with peanut butter breath and no regrets.

My stereo was always playing and, if I felt like dancing, I'd head for the kitchen. The refrigerator door was my partner. I'd just open and close the door so I could swing back and forth. Mr. Kelvinator was one cool guy.

While driving on an interstate highway, I heard the song "Hearts" on my car radio. At that time, it was in the top ten on the charts. Marty Bolin was the vocalist and my son was the drummer. As I kept driving, the song began to fade as the radio signal got weaker. Since I was alone in the car with no one to ask me what the hell I was doing, I pulled over onto the shoulder and drove slowly in reverse till the radio signal became stronger again. Even though I had my own copy of the song at home, this was different. This was like being live in Carnegie Hall on Route 264.

If I am alone and act weird and nobody sees me, am I weird?

17

THE PARKAY VS THE LAND O'LAKES LITANY

"There'll be no oleomargarine in this house!!!"

I heard this from a man who grew up in the same Depression I did. What is this?? Here I am quitting college and designing tombstones for seventy-five cents an hour so we could have butter on the table, while he's staying in college to get that degree because he'd be the breadwinner of the family. (That was the mentality of the forties.)

I remember when I was a little girl; oleo was not the color of butter. It looked like Crisco until it was mixed with a packet of orange powder. That was my job. When I finished kneading it and playing with it, we had butter. I had fun and it was kinda like constructive recreation. Everybody's toast benefited from my fun time. It was like Silly Putty, only it benefited mankind. My ex-husband never knew what he missed as a kid. I can't tell you how many times my husband would say to me or to anyone who would listen, "No matter how poor my family was, we always had real butter on the table."

Every time he brought that up, I'd always think of what my grandmother used to say when she'd hear bragging: "Big front! Hundred dollar suit and torn underwear!"

Now that I'm single again, it's back to oleo. Not that I'm an oleophile. It's within my budget and it's not so terrible. Anyway, I know I'll be going out to dine every so often and there'll be real butter on the table.

PLAYING GAMES WITH MA BELL

Age has no effect on women when it comes to answering the phone.

It starts in their teens. It must be in their genes, because all women have this innate skill. It's just like riding a bike. It all comes back.

Women know just how long it should ring before they answer. Of course, no one ever sees them by the phone chanting their mantra, "Please God, let it be him!" Then they jump right in, pick up the phone, and know how to sound busy, bored, or breathless. It will never be a lost art. It's a woman thing.

Now, obscene calls are something else. They are unnerving and creepy. Women either cry, gasp, or hang up and pray he won't call back. Other women found out that cussing the caller just gets the juices flowing, and the pervert will ring right back.

A friend of mine refused to let anyone harass her that way. She handled it with such relish and delight, the caller hung up. She ruined his day! Gutsy woman!

I'm afraid I'm not cut from the same cloth. I wanted to be "I am woman! Hear me Roar!" But that wasn't going to happen. I was the gasper who took the phone off the hook until someone told me to keep a whistle by the phone. In the event I was ever to get an obscene call, I was to blow the whistle full blast into the phone and deafen the caller. Talk about poetic justice! I am a freelance interpreter for the deaf and he might end up as one of my clients. Talk about power! Now hear me roar!

GIVE ME CREDIT OR GIVE ME DEATH!

Bra burnings were not my cup of tea. I was Adam's rib—not Women's Lib. I never questioned household finances because my husband took care of all of that. I was a real domestic ninnie.

When I was married, everything was in my husband's name. Telephone, electricity, and credit cards: just to name a few. Even my women's magazine subscriptions were in his name. This was a way of life with my generation and totally acceptable.

After my divorce, when I tried to buy a hide-away-bed payable at the end of ninety days, I was turned down because I had no credit rating. I wasn't prepared for the groveling and begging I would go through to get credit.

My husband had excellent credit, but I had none, even though I worked and helped pay the bills. I was the original anonymous donor.

Then I got mad and insisted on speaking with the credit manager. I reassured him that I had a job and that this bill would be paid in ninety days with no problem. He kept mumbling something about rules and single women with no credit rating. He was totally inept and useless. If he were a horse, I would have shot him on the spot.

I remembered when I went looking for my very first job and was turned down because I had no experience. How was I going to get experience and prove myself if I wasn't given a job? It was the same with credit. How could I prove I could pay my bills if I didn't have credit? It was a real Catch 22!

After being turned down so many times in so many places, paranoia set in. Maybe my husband snitched on me when I went over the limit one month. There was no end to humiliation in my quest for credit.

Applying for a credit card was an even more humbling experience. I was told I had to build up a credit rating, but I didn't know how or where to start. Finally, the manager of the bank where I did business came up with an idea. I was given a VISA card with a twenty-five dollar limit and told to use it to buy ten dollars worth of gas every month, making sure my bill was paid on time. I had to do this for a year and, then, I could get approved for a five hundred dollar limit. It was degrading, but I did it. The plastic money predicament makes one do strange things.

Since that time, I've bought a house, three new cars, and have an eight thousand dollar credit line on my credit card.

Remembering all those turn downs, I knew someday my day would come if I waited long enough. After seventeen years, I received a personal invitation to become a member of the American Express family because of my excellent credit rating.

Now it was my turn. I was drunk with power as I thumbed my nose at their offer and told them I was "leaving home without it."

Belatedly, I salute all the Maidenforms that went up in flames, making it possible for me to be a real, genuine, card-carrying big spender!

WHADDYA MEAN I NEED A NEW TRANSMISSION???

Hertz was in first place. Avis came in second by *trying harder*, and Budget-Rent-A-Car followed as a close third. Then Alamo started coming down the stretch with Thrifty, Payless, and Rent-A-Wreck not far behind. Now it's anybody's horse race.

Do you want a Mercedes or do you want to go the cheapie route? There are all kinds of options these days. Competition is stiff. Hertz is no longer number one, but have I got a deal for them that they can't refuse!

"Diversify—rent a guy!" I say.

Mr. Hertz says, "There are escort services for that."

To which I reply, "Mr. Hertz, I am not finished talking. Hear me out. The escort services have the pretty boys, the male models, the Italian stallions, and the Chippendale dancers..

"I don't want to dance till dawn. I want a man with certain skills. Not dancers or wooers. I want a master mechanic.

"All agencies advertise rentals by the day, week, or month; I just want to rent for only an hour or two.

"When I, alone as a single woman, go to any garage to have my air-conditioning checked, I may only need more freon. Nine chances out of ten, I'll be told my compressor's bad. Here's where my rental comes in. He's not only a master mechanic. He's my guardian angel. He'll set 'um straight. The economics of this deal can't be beat. He's cheaper than the seven hundred dollar repair bill for work that didn't need to be done. Not only have I saved money, but also you'll be back on top making more money with this innovation.

"More women get screwed in car repair shops than in the bedroom. No more will the single women of America have to wear old clothes to draw pity, or do ten laps around the rosary beads while waiting to hear the verdict from the service manager.

"Everybody wants to be a hero. Here's your chance! Not only can you be a hero, but also you can be a *rich* hero! Didn't I say I had a deal you just can't refuse?"

NO OUIJA BOARDS FOR ME

I realized I was in pretty bad shape when I picked up the daily paper, bypassed news of world affairs, and went straight to the horoscope section.

One day, I read, "Though intellectually you are on your toes, you are physically and financially on your fanny. Lines of communication tangle. Your cycle is low on the last day. Fold!" Boy! Tell me something I didn't know.

The next day, my horoscope wasn't any better. In the same vein, it went on to say, "Your cycle is low. Your planet Venus continues to trip through that part of your chart that represents emotional drive, sex, and romance. This week, the spirit is willing, but the flesh is weak. Fatigue fades on the last day." Yeah, for me and everybody else who was born between June 21st and July 22nd.

I decided to forget these stargazer generalities that could apply to anyone. I wanted the personal touch. Even Nancy Reagan had her own astrologer. However, the best I could do was a palm reader who could tell me my future for five bucks.

When my eyes got used to the dimly lit room, I found myself sitting across from a woman with a shoebox full of bottles of pills by her side. After staring at my palm for a few minutes, she told me she had to take her medicine because she had bad nerves. She washed down a couple of pills with a Dr. Pepper and then started rambling on about a tall, handsome man in my future. Then she took another pill, drank some more Dr. Pepper, and started telling me very personal, intimate details about the no-good, tall, dark sonofabitch in her life and what she was going to do to him the next time she saw him again. I just realized I blew five bucks to find out about *his* future!

Having learned nothing from this experience, I found myself driving to a nursing home with a friend who insisted we had to visit this quaint little old English lady who was living there and was reputed to be quite a fortuneteller. I should have been tipped off when I found out her fee was a can of Vienna sausages and two packs of Camels. I couldn't believe I slipped to this. I went from a pill poppin' palm reader to a little old lady with lungs like a coal miner and cholesterol lining the entire roadway system of her body. I must've been nuts. It didn't take us long to find out that Miss Great Britain was not on speaking terms with reality.

Since then, I've decided to let the future take care of itself. No more crystal balls or hocus-pocus for me. However, if I can walk on the sidewalk without stepping on a crack, there's going to be a tall handsome man in my future.

MAKE SURE THE PLEASURE OUTWEIGHS THE PAIN

When Ponce De Leon was searching for the Fountain of Youth, he took a wrong turn and found Florida instead. Ponce! Even though you never found the springs, your King Ferdinand would've loved the climate and added years to his life. The senior citizens and retirees of Florida thank you!

Women have known for centuries that the secret to eternal youth is to lie a lot. The wealthier ones get facelifts. Biological clocks can't be stopped from ticking, but the aging process can be slowed down. There's this powerful desire to live longer looking better. When I spent my first winter in Florida, I found it crawling with rich widows and divorcees going to the fountain of *nip and tuck.* There's blepharoplasty, body contouring through liposuction and facelifts.

I thought maybe I should get a facelift. I'm a mature divorced woman. I wasn't rich, but I could save up for it. I decided to see what I'd look like before I went under the knife. I lay on my bed and hung my head over the side so I'd be facing the ceiling. All the loose flesh raced from my jowls to my eyes and I got all squinty. I looked like a cross between Rosalind Russell and a kid with her pigtails pulled too tight. This type of research was giving me bad data, so I pitched it. Instead of being an old broad, I wanted to be a classy looking old dame. *I'd* know I was old, but I'd look great. Then I thought why not be an informer and let the FBI or the government change my whole face at no cost to me. The only expenditures would be running a tab at the local drug store for valium, because, even though I know my face would be great, my nerves would be shot.

In the cosmetic surgery brochure, it is stated that carefully camouflaged incisions are made at the temple, hairline, in the back of the neck above the hairline, and in front of and directly behind the ear.

If I went ahead and got a facelift, what a web I'd have to weave if I ever met Mr. Right. If he ran his hand through my hair after kissing me, he'd see those teeny-weeny telltale scars. Then he'd ask, "What happened here?" I'd try selling him on the idea that one wintry New England day when I was a kid, I got hit by a Flexible Flyer that ran amok. And I got runners on both sides of my head. If he doesn't know what a Flexible Flyer is, then I know he is too young for me.

Confusion, like God, is everywhere. I don't know if I can go through with it. What to do? Everybody always talks about people who have had a facelift. I think I might be too sensitive. I can't stand people talking about me.

I wish I'd paid more attention in my high school chemistry class. I could have come up with a new formula—painless, affordable, industrial strength makeup—something along the line of Sears Weather Beater paint. I'd market it for all those women who can't stand pain or are on limited budgets. This would be their alternative.

I'd become very rich. Then I'd go get a facelift. Damn the torpedoes! Let 'em talk!

STICK-UM THERAPY

To get back self-esteem and self-confidence after a broken marriage or relationship, therapists teach you how to feel good about yourself. One of their techniques is *mirror therapy.* They figure since you look into the bathroom mirror first thing in the morning, last thing at night, and anytime in between, that this is the ideal place to post those yellow stick-um notes with messages you write to yourself for reinforcement. They're in the vein of *God don't make junk, I'm o.k., you're o.k.,* et al.

There is a processing that goes on with this posting of notes to your self. At first, it's the *that's his loss syndrome,* and so, you write it on note #1.

When he let me go, he was suffering from an acute cerebral rectal inversion!

Convincing yourself this is true, note #2 says *He ain't worth the powder to blow him to hell.*

Now the processing gets into the anger stage and note #3 says: *I hope he gets a permanent non-stop itching rash and lives to be 100!*

Now when the processing goes into the philosophical stage, you know you are seeing daylight as note #4 says: *It wouldn't have worked anyway.*

You've got a handle on it when note #5 says: *Life goes on and I'm going to be just fine.*

Those notes are just the highlights. Many notes written in between create another problem—not with your self-esteem, but how you look.

There're so many damn notes on the mirror, you can't see to put on your make-up. Trying to put your make-up on using a compact mirror the size of a half-dollar could run you the risk of ending up looking like *trick or treat.* So that helps goad your processing into an upward swing and down come the notes. If you remove the negative ones first, you're making progress. When you leave note #5 up, you're home free.

The true test is when you run into him again and you can manage to be very poised and pleasant. However, you're only human. You can't resist one more thought. As you stand there, in your mind, you're picturing a yellow stick-um note on his forehead that paraphrases that old Irish blessing: *May you be on your honeymoon a half hour before your prostate kicks out.*

You smile. He thinks you're not mad anymore and smiles back. You're both happy. Everybody wins, unless that Irish blessing which is really a homemade curse, works!

WOMEN AND DRUGS

They're too easy to get. They can be found on every corner in a drug store—Dextrin, Ultra-Slim Fast, Ayds. You name 'em; they got 'em. These over-the-counter magic potions are guaranteed to bring women such euphoria like they've never experienced when they go from a size 14 to a size 10. They'd be so high, they'd be hunting ducks with a rake.

There are pushers in the media getting into America's living rooms—big guns like Tony Lasorda with the hard sell approach yelling, "If I can do it, you can do it, too!"

Then there's the subliminal pusher like Oprah Winfrey who just wheels out sixty pounds of fat in a little red wagon and says nothing. She just lets everybody see what can be expected from her drug of choice.

Women of America, if you're tired of the yo-yo syndrome of breathtaking highs and black depression caused by weight losses and gains, fight back. Taper off with methadone (Nutri-systems, Weight Watchers, Overeaters Anonymous).

Nutri-systems does your thinking for you, with daily menus of pre-packaged meals prepared for you.

Weight Watchers has cheerleaders as motivational speakers at their weekly support group meeting.

Overeaters Anonymous pray a lot and try to stay away from these drugs that didn't live up to their claims. The hard core cases go cold turkey and have their jaws wired shut.

However, there is a drug free program that is offered every five years with an iron-clad guarantee. It's called *Getting In Shape For Your High School Reunion.* There is no stronger motivational force than this. Wipe out cellulite without drugs by walking, running, exercising, and starving yourself to lose twenty-five pounds in three months.

If you don't have that much time, get a divorce—guaranteed to drop twenty pounds overnight. If you're a sensitive person, ditch this idea, because you'll find out when you get to your class reunion, more of your classmates will sit with you if you are a widow than if you're a divorcee. Who wants to feel like a skunk at a lawn party? So be drug free! Eat, drink, and be yourself.

I GOT THOSE WASH DAY BLUES

As a young girl, I remember that laundry was always done on Monday. It was unheard of to wash clothes on any other day of the week. Since the dryer wasn't invented yet, everything you owned was washed and hung out on the clothesline for your neighbors and all the world to see.

I don't know if all the women in New England followed this ritual, but I remember my grandmother and my aunt sticking faithfully to a hard and fast rule about the order of clothes hanging.

Sheets were always hung up on the first line. All the bras, slips, and panties were well hidden by being hung on the second line, and backed up by towels, shirts, pants and dresses on the third line.

Now, with this kind of mentality instilled in me, I dreaded my first trip to the laundromat after having been used to doing laundry in the privacy of my own home for twenty-five years. Since my ex-husband was awarded custody of the washer and dryer, I had no choice.

Then I remembered hearing that singles groups aren't the only places that have single men. They're in laundromats, too. I could get my clothes clean and meet a clean-cut guy at the same time. This could be fun.

On my first trip to the laundromat, everything went smoothly until I started folding my laundry. I shook my pillowcase out and saw my bra fly through the air and land on the pants leg of a very handsome man at the next dryer. The static electricity in the bra just kept it there. Knowing that terrycloth had great traction, I grabbed a dishtowel and swooped down on the bra with it. Then I pretended I was picking it up from the floor.

He never felt a thing. He never knew what happened, and so we never met. Maybe there'd be a next time. But when? Which day? Too bad laundry isn't still done only on Mondays.

THE AGONY AND THE ECSTACY

When I got divorced so late in life, I felt my life was over. My children were practically grown and I didn't quite know what to do with myself. I wasn't ready for Shady Acres, but I wasn't ready for that strange new world of singles, either. So time passed.

After the dust settled from my divorce, well-meaning friends asked if I thought about dating again. I agonized over it and decided against it. More time passed. Then I found out how deep my rut was when I realized I'd rather have a cat and deal with a fur ball than go out on a date.

It was time to get a life. I got out and about. It happened! I was asked for a date. I said "yes" and then thought I must be nuts! I drove myself crazy with thoughts like *I'm a little long in the tooth for all of this-- I'll hide my AARP magazines when he comes to pick me up-- Do I kiss him on the first date?-- I feel like a wrinkled teenager!*

Too much pressure! I was ready to call and cancel. When I looked down at the back of my hand while I was dialing his number, I saw a few liver spots. I figured he might think they were misplaced freckles and find that kinda cute. If I waited too long and the liver spots multiplied, I'd look like a Dalmatian and then my chances would really slim down.

I hung up and told myself to be confident and make sure that when he came to the door, I didn't look like a deer on the highway staring into a set of headlights on high beams.

I was ecstatic to learn that night that I wasn't nuts. I learned that the first date is the hardest at *any* age.

I'D RATHER CHEW ALUMINUM FOIL!

I was twenty-one when I had my first blind date. I was told he was 6' 2" and had blonde, curly hair and blue eyes. Well, those stats were true, but certainly not the whole picture. The unknown factors were the killers! The unknowns were that all his teeth were fighting to get out front (what an overbite!) and his ears were like handles on a trophy cup. I was also told he was a barrel of laughs and lots of fun. I soon found out this nebulous piece of information meant I had a "frat rat" on my hands who could consume a barrel of beer, and his idea of having fun was burping college cheers for the rest of the party. I swore that night never to go on a blind date as long as I lived.

A few years after committing "singlecide" at the age of fifty, I did it again. I guess blind dates are like childbirth—after enough time goes by, you forget the pain.

This time it was an engineer who had worked in Arabia and on the Alaskan pipeline. Very interesting, been everywhere, and had a passion for fine restaurants. I should have been tipped off when I was told he had a great personality. That is one of the major buzzwords in the blind dating game. Now, let's be honest. With these credentials, wouldn't you picture a tall, tanned guy with gray hair, steely eyes, and a "take-charge" air about him?

I'm only 5' 2" and weigh 115 pounds. I was taller than he was and I know I outweighed him. I could tell he had been out of the states a long time when he handed me a corsage the size of a casket spray and just stared at me. We did go on to the "poshest" restaurant in town. But I felt like I was eating with a monk who'd taken the vow of silence. The only saving grace was that he didn't take the vow of poverty or I'd have been stuck with the bill. I know I was born at night, but not *last* night. It didn't take a mental giant to find out that there was no chemistry here. He wasn't too enthralled with me either. I should've had a lobotomy after my first blind date.

Only in the movies are blind dates romantic, adventurous, and exciting, and then lead to marriage except for those few rare cases that were written up in the New England Journal of Medicine under the section pertaining to hormones and chemistry.

Never again! To me, blind dates are an exercise in futility. Kinda like turning on the runway lights for Amelia Earhart.

TALLOW VERSUS VIDEO

Computer date match is for the young and beautiful liars who use embellishment as an art form.

Not me. I stick to the old axiom *Ask and thou shalt receive.* Talk about blind faith!

Whenever I'm in the vicinity of a Catholic church in my travels, I always go in and light a candle at the altar and ask for a Mr. Right in my life. I've lit candles from coast to coast and even lit one in a cathedral in England.

Many of you may not know this, but the burning of Atlanta in *Gone With the Wind* was filmed, not using special effects, but using the flames of the candles I lit looking for Mr. Right.

I remember being in a church in Mill Valley, California, and was nonplussed to see no candles. I saw a woman fussing around the altar and I knew she was a nun in "civvies." With my parochial school upbringing, I can spot a nun a mile away. They never walk. They float. I told her it was my first time in that church, and that I'd never been in a Catholic church without candles. She just smiled and said, "Then make a wish." Then she floated away. I'm sure the brokers on Wall Street are puzzled over the upsurge of church candles over pork bellies. I've almost burned down three churches in my zeal. Now's the time to buy.

If I ever find Mr. Right, that's the time to sell!

IS THERE A DOCTOR IN THE HOUSE?

If we are to be taken in by all the pagers we see on men's belts in a singles' bar, we'd think the American Medical Association was having their convention there.

Not to be impressed. Chances are that these pagers are rentals, and when these guys get beeped and head for the pay phone, they're not calling General Hospital. They're thanking a friend for calling them, and then proceed to give instructions on when to call again in the hopes that they've duly impressed some pretty lady. If their luck holds out, they may be "playing doctor" after closing time

Then there's Mr. Thrifty. He wears his garage door opener on his belt. He never gets paged. He tries to look cool, but doesn't quite make it. The word CRAFTSMAN on the front of the pager was a dead giveaway—a Sears' model yet. He should've at least gone for the GENIE.

THE ROTARY CLUB'S THE PLACE FOR ME.

I never could find a singles' group I could fit into. I was either too young or too old—mostly, the latter. I was divorced six years before I let a co-worker talk me into going with her to one of her group meetings.

It was called SOLOS—an acronym for "Single Ones Loving Others." It was one of the support groups of the Harvey Brown Presbyterian Church. Even though I was an Irish Catholic, I was told everyone was welcome. Hassle-free and full of Christians. Sounded good to me. I wanted to love someone, reach out, and give and get some support.

At the first meeting, the head count was twenty-five women and four men. When I die and come back into the next world, I want to be a man. It's supply and demand. There's a critical shortage of eligible males and a dearth of lonely, vulnerable women.

It seems the only pre-requisites a man had to have was the ability to see lightning and hear thunder! He had his pick of the female group and inevitably veered toward the younger women, knowing they'd go out with him. The odds were in his favor. Unbeatable! He was a scarcity in this group. He never had it so good in his previous life, before he married his first wife. And now, cruel statistics made him a hot commodity even if he was a Cro-Magnon.

Women over fifty were chopped liver. After I'd come home after one of these meetings, I'd find myself lying awake in bed at night listening to my skin go "wrink! wrink! wrink!"

Before my self–esteem and confidence were totally shot, I yelled "uncle" and got out of the group. No one thrives on rejection, so I knew I made the right move.

There's one thing that bugs me, though. I've heard of King Henry the Eighth, John Wesley, and Martin Luther, but who the hell is Harvey Brown???

I WANT A MAIL ORDER BOYFRIEND

Many years ago, the Sears & Roebuck catalog was many things to many people. There was a day when this magnificent illustrated catalog was delivered free of charge to everyone who had an R.F.D. mailing address.

Before the days of *Playboy*, teenage boys peeked at the lingerie pages. Little girls made paper dolls from the men, women, and children's clothing sections. Before Scott Tissue and Charmin, outdated issues were used in the outhouse.

The Christmas issue was the forerunner of the F A O Schwartz catalog and fondly referred to as the "wish book."

You could buy anything—furniture, clothing, yard goods, and tools. If children needed shoes, an outline of their feet traced on paper was sent in with the order. There was no end to the products displayed on pages abounding in color. It was a mail order mall with no parking problems.

Even houses could be bought with plans, lumber, and hardware right down to the last nail.

The Sears catalog is no longer free and the Roebuck name is no longer. But for $5 a book, wouldn't it be great to be able to check out the spring, winter, summer, and fall line of eligible males and send for a mail order boyfriend? Sears needs to add this concept to their overflowing inventory and watch their stock soar.

There are no guarantees in life and there are no guarantees with Computer Date match and Matchmakers International, which have been known to cost consumers hundreds and even thousands of dollars.

Only Sears guarantees satisfaction and refunds if not pleased with your purchase. Dear Mr. Sears, how about it? You've got my $5.00 and I'd like to put my order in right now for the dark haired guy on page 215, Catalog #DM 7545.

STRIKE WHILE THE CASSEROLE'S HOT

For women who want so much to be married again, forget joining singles' groups, skip the ads in the *Personals* section of the classifieds, and don't go on a cruise. Save your energy and save your money.

Go for a widower. It's like shooting fish in a barrel. They are so malleable, and after thirty or forty years of marriage, they can't bear to be alone.

If you should take the plunge, don't worry about bickering after the honeymoon is over. No problem. He had domestic, good-natured or heavy-duty bickering for years with the deceased and thinks it's just a way of life. It'll seem like old times to him—same old action with just a slight change in the cast of characters. He'll jump right back into the fray.

Women who dare not remove tags from mattresses and pillows under penalty of law need not apply. This is not for the faint-hearted.

In tennis terminology, the word *love* means *nothing.* It must also mean nothing to widowers, because so many are back in the church shortly after the funeral, repeating wedding vows to a new mate they hardly know.

Widowers never have a chance to pine away because they are fattened up by the potential brides who come bearing casseroles. I've heard them referred to as the *brisket brigade.* The body of the deceased is warmer than the brisket. This is the oldest ploy in the world and pretty transparent. It's been done since the beginning of time. The only difference was that, in my day, there was a decent waiting period.

I see more creativity and innovation today. Some women bring the widowers self-help books on coping with death, on the pre-text of being a friend and wanting to help him work through his grief.

Other women have been known to call widowers on the phone late at night, offering veiled references to "companionship" and "being there" *any* hour of the day or night.

In Florida, one particular condo complex had women in sexy bathing suits hiding in the elevator, waiting for the new widower to go down to the swimming pool.

Then we have the "compassionate stalkers." If they find out a woman of their acquaintance is in poor health, they get busy doing some advance P.R. for themselves by always dropping by to visit the wife and offering to do anything they can for her. These women make sure they look like a million bucks and only drop by when the husband will be home.

After hearing all these stories, I've come to the conclusion that timing is everything. The bottom line is: Be indispensable! Don't go through all this palaver. Just cut to the chase and give him a ride to the cemetery.

DANCIN' AIN'T NO CAKE WALK THESE DAYS

Everything good is bad—everything bad is good. With suggestive lyrics like these, I figured I didn't stand a chance unless my partner was deaf. What happened to the romantic but safe ballads like "Moonlight Serenade" and "Star Dust?"

Now that I am divorced, how do I get back in the swing of things? Speaking of swing, I remember a dance partner asking me, "Do you swing?"

To which I replied enthusiastically, "I sure do! I'd rather swing than eat!"

(Back in the forties, to swing was to do the swing or jitterbug.)

He lit up like a Christmas tree. I thought I'd found a kindred spirit in the world of Terpsichore. I found out soon enough that he wasn't talking about the Arthur Murray stuff.

Q: Why don't Baptists have sex standing up?

A: So people won't think they're dancing.

They felt dancing was a sin. I wonder if they knew something we didn't know—that in the future, we'd be faced with the Lambada—the new Brazilian dance craze that makes Dirty Dancing look like the Minuet. I saw a talk show segment on TV where dancers of all ages were interviewed in a San Francisco club trying to master the Lambada. They ranged from a fifty year old computer salesman dancing with an instructor, to a girl in her twenties who said, "It's great! There's nothing to it. Just ride your partner's thigh, and he'll do the rest."

I couldn't understand why the computer salesman was paying good money to take lessons. I've danced with men a time or two who were doing the same identical steps, but they had no name for it. I think the Brazilians learned it from us.

WANNA TAKE A CHANCE?

The winds of change are blowing. People no longer have to be married to each other if they want to go to bed together. These are uncharted waters for those of us in that generation who would cleave only to one until death.

After my divorce, the first time I was approached for sex on a date, I didn't know whether to call a cop or box his ears. I wanted him to know that I was more than the sum of my anatomical parts.

Along came Dr. Ruth Westheimer, a noted psycho-sex therapist, summing up her philosophy on sex: *Anything that two consenting adults do in the bedroom, kitchen, or living room is all right.*

As time went on, I found out for myself and from my single friends, that it was nothing to be asked for sex on a date. Then I realized it was not like being married. It's not my conjugal duty. It's my decision, and if I choose not to have sex, I have the right to say "No."

Here are some classic types and responses to the answer *No*.

MACHO MAN: You've never had a *real* man!

MR. BELLIGERENT: You've been married and had kids. It's not like you were a virgin.

THE PROPHET: This will change your life.

THE BULL SHIT ARTIST: We have to do it so I'll know if
we are compatible before we get married.
(This was said after the second date.)

THE MISSIONARY: I only want to help you. You shouldn't be without
sex.

THE SNAKE OIL SALESMAN: I won't do anything you don't want me
to. I guarantee it. (Talks out of two
sides of his mouth—tries to sell you a
bill of goods by saying one thing while
he still pursues his tack of getting to
the bedroom. He retired the trophy for
tenacity.)

MR. NOSEY: When's the last time you had sex?

Now with herpes and AIDS running rampant, I've come to the conclusion
that the only safe sex is gazing at each other across a crowded room.

WHO'S THE BOSS?

I always thought the role reversals came when you were in your seventies. Your children start helping you manage your finances as opposed to when you used to dole out their allowances. They start holding your hand at intersections as opposed to when you used to make them look both ways before crossing the street. They check to see if you are eating the right foods that are good for you as opposed to when you used to make them eat all their vegetables because it was good for them. In these flashbacks, I was the boss.

I remember worrying about my two sons dating nice girls and I would tell them there was nothing wrong with virginity and curfews. (My New England upbringing spills over on to my kids.) They brought their girlfriends home to meet me.

Now, after being divorced fourteen years, I found myself consulting with my boys about a widower I had met. I wanted to know what they thought if I took trips with him. Up until that time, the only trips I ever took were guilt trips and I had a round trip ticket. I always felt badly about the divorce and the two boys being caught in the middle.

I grew up with the Mom, the American flag, and apple pie mentality. I cherished my boys' love and respect and asked them if they'd think any less of me. This was a real role reversal!

See how out of touch I am? You ask the guy if he will think any less of you—not your kids!

AT MY AGE, I DON"T BUY GREEN BANANAS, HE SAYS

The philosophy of biological clocks ticking on is no longer a female notion. There are some sixty and seventy year old men out there who are subscribing to that theory, also. They claim their sex drive is in overdrive because they feel they are living on borrowed time.

Clinical data has shown that men between the ages of eighteen and thirty-five think of sex six times an hour. In the next fifteen years or so, it is about three or four times in an hour. As the years pass, it dwindles, but never dies.

Age is no barrier when it comes to sex. There is no cut off date. If he's breathing, he's sexually active.

I pictured sixty and seventy year olds as mild mannered and shy until some of my single friends dating senior citizens regaled me with some hair-raising tales ranging from no time for seduction to attempted geriatric rape. (There is also no age barrier for girl talk.)

A very beautiful widow, in her sixties, told me about meeting a seemingly wonderful man in his seventies. She was quite wealthy, but had no cause to worry about his motives because he had a summer home up north and a winter penthouse on Marco Island. They met through mutual friends. The first date was a leisurely dinner at the trendiest restaurant in town, with coffee and brandy back at her place.

The second date was the same scenario, but the pace was picked up at dinner. He ate like he was in a pie-eating contest and wanted to win. Then back to her place for coffee and brandy.

He wasn't there half an hour when, without a word, he pounced on her like a tiger. She became upset and told him to bug off in no uncertain terms, with her voice bordering on hysteria. This alerted her three-pound "tea cup" poodle that became an attack dog that night. She thought her mistress was being hurt and started yipping and nipping at Casanova's pants leg. That put a crimp in the lovemaking, bringing the lovemaking to a screeching halt. No seduction here!

Another story comes to mind concerning a trim, ninety-five pound, vivacious, attractive seventy-five year old widow. Dancing was her favorite pastime. One night she met a man in his sixties at a local V.F.W. Post dance, and they hit it off immediately. She danced every dance with him till closing time.

A few afternoons later, he surprised her by showing up on her doorstep and asking if he could come in and visit for a while. They sat in her living room and made small talk about their backgrounds, hobbies, interests, and grandchildren.

Then, with no warning at all, he picked her up and carried her into her bedroom. She was wiry, but not that strong. She began to hit him and asked what he was trying to do. He muttered something about, even though they were both older, spontaneity was a wonderful thing.

She then replied, "I can't believe I'm being raped by a grandfather!"

That deflated his sails, among other things.

When some sexy senior citizen comes on to you against your wishes, don't think that closing your eyes, clicking your heels twice, and quoting Dorothy *I want to go home* is gonna get it.

You've got to be firm, with a no-nonsense, no-frills *NO!* If he's wearing a hearing aid, reach over, turn up the volume and let him have it! When these men act like they are making a last ditch effort at life with their hi-jinks libido, remember what Lou Pinella, manager of the Cincinnati Reds said: "You gotta have a certain demeanor—de meaner, de better."

I've come to the conclusion that Geritol must be one helluva tonic. It's not only for iron in your blood. It's really an aphrodisiac!!!!

THERE"S NO SUCH THING AS A FREE LUNCH, AND DINNER HAS ITS PRICE, TOO.

Years ago, pickled pigs feet, hardboiled eggs in a jar, jawbreaker pretzels, and peanuts in the shell were yours for the taking when you'd belly up to the bar for a drink. No extra charge. What a treat! Play your cards right and you had a free lunch. Macho h'ors douvres!

The more sophisticated, updated version of this is today's "Happy Hour." From 4 pm to 6 pm or thereabouts, with the purchase of a drink, you can find anything from bowls of dip, large cheese balls, deep-fried veggies, bite size pizza, to buffalo wings for the taking. If you load up your plate a few times, that can be dinner. Still free.

When it comes to a legitimate dinner with a menu and a male escort, sometimes it can be a different story. Not free. There are some men who think foreplay is buying you dinner.

I remember being in a very elegant restaurant with a man whose dinner dialogue was bugging me before we were through with our appetizers. He kept kidding about us skipping the dessert menu and having dessert at his place or mine. (I knew there was no dessert in my refrigerator!)

I called the waiter over and told him I wanted separate checks at the end of the meal. My date sputtered and choked and insisted I was his guest. I refused and said that, now that I was paying for my own dinner, I could enjoy my meal without any more hassle from him. I owed him nothing.

However, trying to make a point stinks! I overextended myself on my VISA, and, with the money he saved, he was back out there on the Duncan Hines circuit, doing his dessert rap with somebody else. Nothing changes.

NOAH WEBSTER AND I ARE IN THE DARK

Herpes—a Greek god

Sexual freedom—you don't have to pay for it

Sexual revolution—battle of the sexes

Missionary position—how your preacher stands on a certain issue

Consenting adults—grownups giving children permission to go on field trips, et al

Threesome—what you get in golf when you can't get a foursome

Menage a trios—a French dessert

Swing—dance (verb): a seat suspended by a rope hanging from a tree limb (noun)

G-spot—alphabetical parking space

One night stand—a piece of furniture found next to the bed

Oral sex—chatting while making love

Indecent exposure—lousy film

What do I know? In my day, there was no trendy terminology applied to every facet of sex. I don't understand the new jargon that has come about since my wedding day.

After my divorce, I felt like Rip Van Winkle, only I'd been asleep just twenty-five years. I was safe in my predictable, marital cocoon. I'm older, but no wiser when it comes to living in a more enlightened sexual era.

One thing I *do* know—we've come a long way from the Puritan era when a mother would tell her daughter on her wedding night, "Lie back and think of England."

MEN I'VE DATED, ALMOST DATED, AND NEVER DATED. THANK GOD!

THE HOLOGRAM—go to a party with him and watch him appear, disappear, and reappear.

THE MAGICIAN—The Great Houdini couldn't hold a candle to this guy when it came to vanishing acts.

MR. TIME WARP—wears polyester leisure suits, still plays canasta, and drives an Edsel guaranteed to give you a detached retina.

OLD MCDONALD—his zip code is EE--i—ee—i—o and so's his whole life.

THE STAR GAZER—he asks, "What's your sign?" and is slightly round shouldered from all the gold chains around his neck.

THE MILWAUKEE TUMOR—he has a large growth in the belly area and you can always count on a pitcher of beer to be the *drink du jour.*

THE OCTOPUS—the guy with eight hands whom everybody has met at one time or another in their lives. Need I say more?

THE RHODES SCHOLAR—he's always deep in thought and he never lets you in on it. You're not smart enough.

THE GOVERNMENT MULE—he eats like one and is living proof that the way to a man's heart is through his stomach.

THE JOCK—he can be seen bringing a six-pack of beer to any woman who'll let him in her living room to watch sporting events on TV till her clothes go out of style.

MR. MONOTONE—you can never tell whether he's having a good time or not.

ECONO MAN—he splits the bill with his date if he can get away with it.

GOOD OLD BOY—he wears a belt buckle the size of dinner plate that tears up your stomach on the dance floor.

VELCRO LIPS—you do all the talking, He has nothing to say. Makes for a long evening.

PINOCCHIO—he tells so many lies, his nose should be three feet long.

TOO GOOD TO BE TRUE—he is! He's married.

It takes all kinds to make a world, I guess. In all fairness to all the really great guys in the world, I know you're out there. But where? You've got a great hiding place. As we used to say when we were kids playing hide and seek, "Come out, come out, wherever you are!"

MAY—DECEMBER LOGIC

How about these statistics? A *zillion* women and a million men. For men, the world is pretty much their candy store when it comes to dating. This is pretty heady stuff for some of these guys who couldn't get a date in high school. Now there are plenty of lonely women out there who would jump at the chance to go out with them today, even though they look like Godzilla.

Older men have been going out with younger women for years. They used to be called *sugar daddies* and they were rich. Today, older men don't have to be rich. They can get younger women to go out with them because the ratio's undeniably in their favor.

Traditionally, older women rarely went out with younger men. Now, since men their own age aren't dating them, they are resorting to seeking younger men and finding they are liking it. They also notice now that an old man's pants never fit right, they have no behinds, and they always have to go to the bathroom.

It's a known fact that most women outlive men, so dating a younger man isn't such a bad idea. When his time comes, the woman will also be about ready to cash in her chips, and they can hold hands and jump into the grave together.

HEY! I WAS JUST KIDDING!

Love is lovelier the second time around.
Familiar lyrics?
The next song that comes to mind is *Love and marriage, love and marriage, go together like a horse and carriage.*
The deduction drawn from these two songs would be that if love is lovelier the second time around, so is marriage.
One way to avoid the pitfalls of another marriage going sour is to keep tuned in for verbal clues that telegraph what's ahead.
Here's some sample dialogue that sends up a red flag:

SHE: We've been invited to Tom and Sally's wedding. Want to go?
HE: Sure. Why not? I've never missed a hangin' yet.

SHE: You never say you love me anymore.
HE: I don't have to say it. I asked you to marry me, didn't I?

SHE: I heard Dick and Ann are getting a divorce. Isn't that sad?
HE: I'll tell you what's sad. Alimony…that's the screwin' you get for all the screwin' you got.

SHE: Did you hear that Jack gave Beverly an engagement ring?
HE: Yeah, that's how it starts. First, it's the engagement ring; then it's the wedding ring; Then it's the suffering!

Only kidding? Remember the old axiom: *Many a truth is spoken in jest!*
Buzz words to listen for when he refers to his friends' wives: *the ball and chain, the old lady, the battleaxe, the warden, and the war department*—just to name a few.

DIVORCE AFTER FIFTY AIN'T NO DISGRACE, BUT IT AIN'T NO HONOR EITHER

You don't need a comedian like this unless his name is Henny Youngman, who is famous for his night club act opening line: *Take my wife—please!* At least he's making money with this type of humor and he'll never divorce you. Without a wife, he's got no act!

POWER STRUGGLES 101

The dissonance of men and women is unbelievable when it comes to restaurants, toilets, map reading and much more.

To a woman, the three most exciting words that sound like a thousand violins ringing in her ears are *Let's eat out*. Dining out from a male perspective and a female perspective is totally different. He wants substance; she wants atmosphere. He likes to eat. She likes to dine. A Big Mac and a quiche are worlds apart. Men and women just don't think alike.

The bathroom is the battleground for the sexes till the day they die. Women complain about men leaving the toilet seat up. They feel men should leave the toilet seat down in deference to them because they do not stand up to pee. Men feel the seat should be left up because they do. This is a deadlock that will never be resolved unless it can be proven that a woman could drown if she fell in.

The number one reason for divorce is neither money nor sex as everyone would believe. It's map reading. Men and women have been locked in mortal combat and have heaped verbal abuse on each other from how to read a map to folding it back to its original state. It's justifiable for a man to explode after asking his wife how far it is to Louisville and hearing her say, "Oh, about half an inch, or as long as my thumbnail." However, I think he's just as unreasonable when he asks what the mileage is to the next town and gets annoyed when she takes too long to answer and then says, "Wait a minute. I'm still counting." You could go blind with those microscopic numbers that can hardly be seen with the naked eye. Men may be better map-readers, but, by dam, they can't fold them and get them back into the glove compartment. They lack the basic skills of folding diapers, tablecloths, and sheets, too.

There's a lesson to learned here in PS 101. There's no end to power struggles. They just go on and on with a lot of compromising. So, I say it's a global thing. World powers do it. Men and women do it. I wonder if birds and bees do it?

BOOB TUBE POWER

Charlie Brown says, "Them that's got the gold makes the rules."

I say, "Them that has charge of the remote control for the TV has the ultimate power in a marriage."

I was married in 1984 and two years later, the first NFL game was televised. Then it was Orange Bowls, Rose Bowls, Sugar Bowls, and on and on.

In the days before remote control, there was more interaction in the power struggle over what to watch on TV. The husband usually watched the game prone on the couch. He would doze. The wife would tiptoe up to the TV and change the channel. Some sixth sense would alert the husband and he would say, "I'm watching the game! Don't change the channel" The wife's retort would be, "You were sleeping." The classic reply would be, "I was not. I was just resting my eyes."

It was a cat and mouse game. You'd win a few and lose a few, but, at least, you had a shot at it.

I was divorced before the age of the remote, so I can't speak from my own marital experience. However, when visiting my married friends, I never saw the wife operating the remote control if the husband was in the same room. The "Remote Commando" (the husband) would inevitably zap everyone through a dizzying array of programs every time a commercial came on. Sometimes another program would be more appealing and then every one forgot what they had been watching. I never knew how anything ended. It was nerve-wracking!

When George Bernard Shaw's wife was asked why she was always knitting in the presence of her husband and his friends, she replied, "I like to keep my hands busy so that I won't reach over and choke him every time he tells the same stories over and over."

I think if the remote control had been in popular use during my marriage, I'd have taken up knitting or gotten divorced sooner.

HOW NOT TO BE THE DUMPEE

At the beginning of every relationship, a man pays as close attention to you as he would to a cross-eyed javelin thrower. You are wined and dined—a single rose here—a sentimental note there—phone calls as lengthy as those made by a teenager who has her own phone. There is no end to the excitement.

Eventually, this levels out to the "comfort zone" where it's not as euphoric, but it's nice. Then, somehow, there's trouble in paradise and he says things like, "This isn't working" or "I never meant to hurt you" or "I'd still like us to be friends, even though I want to end this relationship." *Ya-te-ta, ya-ye-ta, ya.* And so it goes.

You're never too old to hurt when you get dumped. No one thrives on rejection. Whether you're the dumper or the dumpee, there's pain. More so if you're the dumpee. Ego is a fragile thing.

There's an old saying: *When life hands you lemons, make lemonade.* If you have been dumped, the best way to heal your bruised ego is to turn around and make some lemonade. Become the dumper!

Arrange to go out for one last dinner with him. Just tell him it's for old times' sake and to show there are no hard feelings. Order the most expensive meal on the menu and, after you've eaten your last bite, look him straight in the eye and say, "This wasn't such a good idea after all. I just realized sitting across from you this entire meal that I don't even like you."

Dab your lips with a napkin, leave the table, and hail a cab. It's a great feeling, even though it's only a temporary rush. You may still feel like hell when you get home, but you can always tell your friends, "I dumped him!"

A PEEVE BY ANY OTHER NAME
STILL DRIVES ME NUTS

The expression "pet peeve" is a paradox. How can any peeve be a *pet* peeve when that's what drives you crazy in the first place? A peeve is a peeve is a peeve.

When I was married, I had no pets or favorites. All mine were "dependable" peeves. They could be counted on to happen with regularity.

My husband would come from work and I would ask, "Anything exciting happen today?" and he would say, " N-a-ah, same old, same old." The next door neighbor drops in and my husband would launch into this great story about how there was a bomb scare at work, his secretary fainted, the building had to be evacuated, and on and on.

Toilet water can be sweet and toilet water can be ice cold. The sweet stuff I dabbed behind my ears. The cold stuff I immersed my behind in, if I wasn't looking, because he always left the toilet seat up.

Now here's a universal peeve. I've never met a woman whose husband would ask for directions when he got lost. There are men who would drive till they needed an oil change before they would ask for directions.

One time I had a date with a man who told me he wouldn't lick his thumb to turn pages in a doctor's waiting room because he was afraid there would be germs in the magazines left by other patients. His hypochondria peeved me and I never saw him again.

You know what really peeves me? I left all the old familiar peeves behind only to find out there are all kinds of peeves out there—enough to go around for everyone. There's no escape from "peevedom!"

I've been divorced thirty years and the beat goes on and the peeves keep coming. Times have changed and so have the peeves. As I look back on my marriage, my peeves were just a minor irritant in comparison to the peeves cropping up in the dynamics of living in today's world.

For starters, here's a couple from telephone hell. There's a fungus among us, and it's spreading like wildfire. It's called *free long distance minutes into infinity!* It seems these minutes must be used up before the next month's billing by the cell phone company. One night while watching TV, I received a call from a former shipmate from World War II. I hadn't heard from her in years. After about an hour, I suggested bringing the call to a close and that I could call her another time on my nickel.

She assured me that wasn't a problem. She was using her daughter's free minutes and kept right on talking. I was beginning to wonder if her daughter had any friends.

Now we come to the biggest lie ever told. *Hi! I know you're busy, so I'll keep this short.* That never happens. You're dealing with a telephone maven with amazing breath control—she never takes one, so you can't jump in. Another verbal ploy is *oh, one more thing before I forget.* That's another lie. It's *not* one more thing. She's got an agenda that would choke a horse. I know one thing. I'm going to have to change my hair style to cover that cauliflower ear I've developed.

And then there's the promise peeve. You're at a cocktail party and the person you're talking to says, "I'll be right back." Never happens. You begin to think the ball got stuck on your deodorant stick.

Who hasn't heard that open ended sentence: *Let's do lunch?* The next line should be: *I'll have my people call your people.* Then I wouldn't feel so wretched when it doesn't happen. I could always blame it on the fact that I have no people.

The weather report can also make me peevish. I need to know the temperature every day so I can dress accordingly. But, that, too, can't be achieved because I keep getting the temperature and the wind chill factor at the airport. What's up with that? I don't live at the airport!

And the beat goes on and the peeves keep coming.

CULINARY DILEMMAS

When I was a bride and a veritable rookie in the kitchen, my husband had me believing that the four basic food groups were meat, potatoes, gravy, and beer.

When we were invited to friends' homes for dinner, he'd invariably compliment the cook on her uses of spices in her meals. (And here we were on the same bottle of tabasco sauce we bought when we set up housekeeping.) What a guy! Then he'd throw me off when he'd rave about a particular dish. So, my next move would be to corner the hostess before the evening was over and get her recipe.

After serving these dishes at home, I found out this was a mistake. He didn't even like these dishes. He said he laid on the praise so she wouldn't notice how much still lay on his plate.

After my divorce, I lost twenty pounds. Part of it was due to the trauma, and I'm sure the other part occurred when I found out what the real four basic food groups really were.

There were dining adventures and rituals ahead of me that I had never experienced. I discovered that when people got together to order Chinese take-out food, each one would order what he'd like to have. We would end up with ten little white cartons of mystery dishes, and then everyone would want to sample everyone else's food or trade. I don't like to eat someone else's Moo Goo Gai Pan or other dishes I've never heard of. If I liked it, I would have ordered it. I don't like to trade. I don't think it's fun. I think it's a pain in the ass.

It's the same with pizza. I always get screwed. All I want is a plain cheese pizza, and everyone else wants to order three kinds of meat, peppers, onions, mushrooms, and anchovies. Anchovies make my tongue swell!

Maybe I need assertiveness training and let the crumbs fall where they may. Or maybe I'm just not a good sport.

Having what I want to have when and how I want to have it makes me feel almost anti-social. My God, I'm even looking back on those pre-divorce basic food groups and thinking *so what if I pick up a few pounds.* Life was much simpler then. And as for spicing up my meals, there's always that twenty-five- year old bottle of aged, mellow tabasco sauce.

NUTS TO THE FRIENDLY SKIES

Picking up my ex-husband at the airport after a business trip meant he'd be regaling me with tales of what a great time he'd had on the plane. The flight attendants were so friendly and such fun, and somehow he always ended up seated next to a pretty girl. He never sat next to an ugly woman. Maybe they weren't allowed on his flights. If there happened to be a man sitting next to him, he would always be the corporate type or some other profession that would generate stimulating conversation throughout the flight.

Until I was divorced, I had flown only twice in the glamorous and fun-filled "Coffee, tea, or me" era. Many years later, after my divorce, my career had me flying all over the country. I remembered the stories my ex-husband had told me and I looked forward to the excitement of sitting next to fascinating people and eating gourmet meals.

Wrong! Times had changed! Instead of a sandwich on a short flight, it was bread sticks or peanuts. And the not-so-exotic meals on a longer flight sent my stomach into gastronomic gymnastics. We'd have been better off if we'd been given begging bowls and sent up to first class. The flight attendants (as they're called today) were no fun at all. All they did was serve food and drinks and spend the rest of the time explaining why our plane was behind schedule.

The passengers I sat next to were nothing like the ones my ex-husband experienced.

I'd get a young service man from Fort Knox who kept whimpering about being shipped to Germany. And we weren't even at war!

Another time, I sat next to a blind woman wearing a black dress, who kept asking me if there were any crumbs on her dress while we were eating lunch.

Then there was a loud mouth employee of a rival airline who griped about the delays, the poor service, and on and on. He was obnoxious, overbearing, and loud. He bitched from the time we took off until we landed. Nothing pleased him. He would have bitched if they hung him with a new rope.

It gets worse. I sat next to a freckled-faced flatulent teenager who wore a Sony Walkman that was so loud, I could hear the fallout spilling out of his ear plugs. He must have subscribed to theory that redundancy was the spice of jive, because I heard the same damn tape for three hours and five minutes.

These are only a few of the adventures I had at thirty thousand feet and above. I've come to the conclusion that single, handsome, exciting, articulate, successful, compassionate, sensitive men with a sense of humor are not allowed on my flights.

THE MENAGERIE METAPHOR MAZE

I have often mused about the difference in menagerie metaphor maze between men and women and its ramifications.

PROBLEM: How do women who are:

cute as a bug's ear   eat like a bird

happy as a lark   purr like a kitten

scared as a rabbit   fuss like a mother hen

graceful as a gazelle   chatter like a magpie

find the man of her dreams when she finds he's

stubborn as a mule   drinks like a fish

sly as a fox   feisty as a banty rooster

eats like a pig   smells like a goat

and acts like a bull in a china shop?

SOLUTION: Women discover that there are also men who are:

loyal as a dog   gentle as a lamb

strong as an ox   work like a horse

have the eye of an eagle and the heart of a lion.

And it has been rumored there are some men who have the memory of an elephant and never forget birthdays, Valentine's Day, Mother's Day, and anniversaries.

VIVE LA DIFFERENCE!

EPILOGUE

A man becomes a shadow when a woman leaves him. I don't remember where I heard this, but I'm including it here just because I like it.

Though not as poetic and thought-provoking, here are some things to think about for all you women who were fifty and older when divorced:

The only thing that likes change is a wet baby.

So many of us don't like change.

Don't harbor anger and bitterness. It makes lines in your face and holes in your stomach.

Be ready for change. You'll love it!

And you'll see. Life goes on.....

Printed in the United States
30587LVS00006B/1-219